# THE RITE OF RENEWAL

### A Rite of Wands Short Story

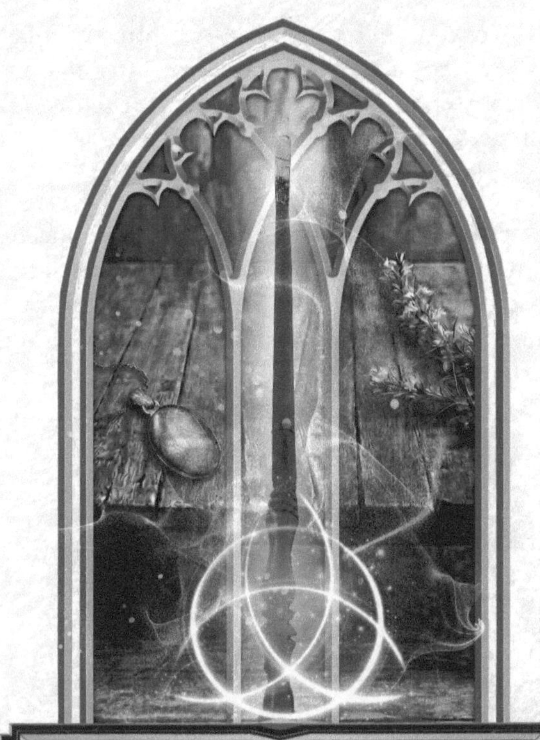

## MACKENZIE FLOHR

# THE RITE OF RENEWAL

Published by Iverna Press, LLC
620 Helen Street | Mount Morris, MI 04858 | USA
www.mackenzieflohr.com
Printed in the United States of America.
ISBN-13: 979-8-9949028-0-6

# THE RITE OF RENEWAL

A RITE OF WANDS SHORT STORY

MACKENZIE FLOHR

To my parents

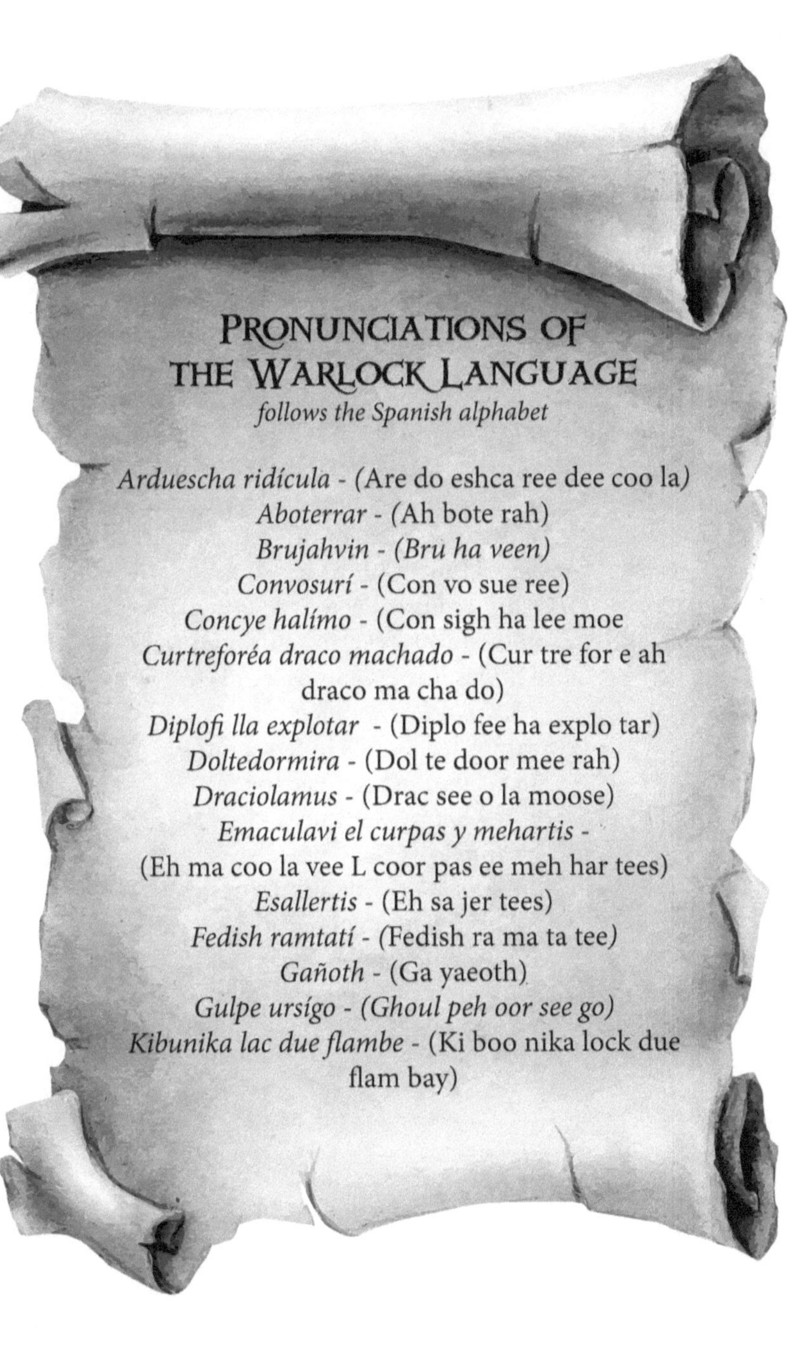

PRONUNCIATIONS OF
THE WARLOCK LANGUAGE
follows the Spanish alphabet

Arduescha ridícula - (Are do eshca ree dee coo la)
Aboterrar - (Ah bote rah)
Brujahvin - (Bru ha veen)
Convosurí - (Con vo sue ree)
Concye halímo - (Con sigh ha lee moe
Curtreforéa draco machado - (Cur tre for e ah
draco ma cha do)
Diplofi lla explotar - (Diplo fee ha explo tar)
Doltedormira - (Dol te door mee rah)
Draciolamus - (Drac see o la moose)
Emaculavi el curpas y mehartis -
(Eh ma coo la vee L coor pas ee meh har tees)
Esallertis - (Eh sa jer tees)
Fedish ramtatí - (Fedish ra ma ta tee)
Gañoth - (Ga yaeoth)
Gulpe ursígo - (Ghoul peh oor see go)
Kibunika lac due flambe - (Ki boo nika lock due
flam bay)

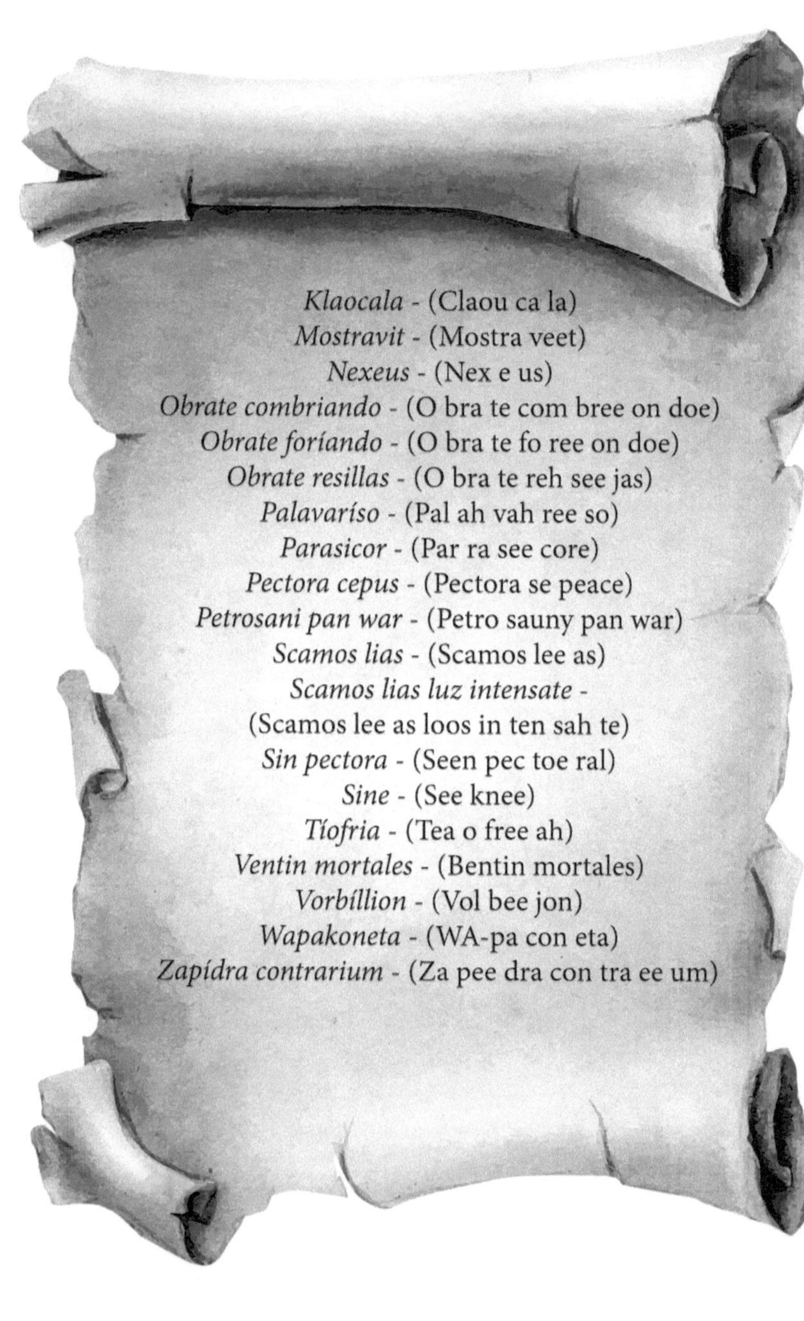


*Klaocala* - (Claou ca la)
*Mostravit* - (Mostra veet)
*Nexeus* - (Nex e us)
*Obrate combriando* - (O bra te com bree on doe)
*Obrate foríando* - (O bra te fo ree on doe)
*Obrate resillas* - (O bra te reh see jas)
*Palavaríso* - (Pal ah vah ree so)
*Parasicor* - (Par ra see core)
*Pectora cepus* - (Pectora se peace)
*Petrosani pan war* - (Petro sauny pan war)
*Scamos lias* - (Scamos lee as)
*Scamos lias luz intensate* -
(Scamos lee as loos in ten sah te)
*Sin pectora* - (Seen pec toe ral)
*Sine* - (See knee)
*Tíofria* - (Tea o free ah)
*Ventin mortales* - (Bentin mortales)
*Vorbíllion* - (Vol bee jon)
*Wapakoneta* - (WA-pa con eta)
*Zapídra contrarium* - (Za pee dra con tra ee um)

*"It doesn't matter what happens in your life;
what matters is how you choose to react to it."*
—Mackenzie Flohr

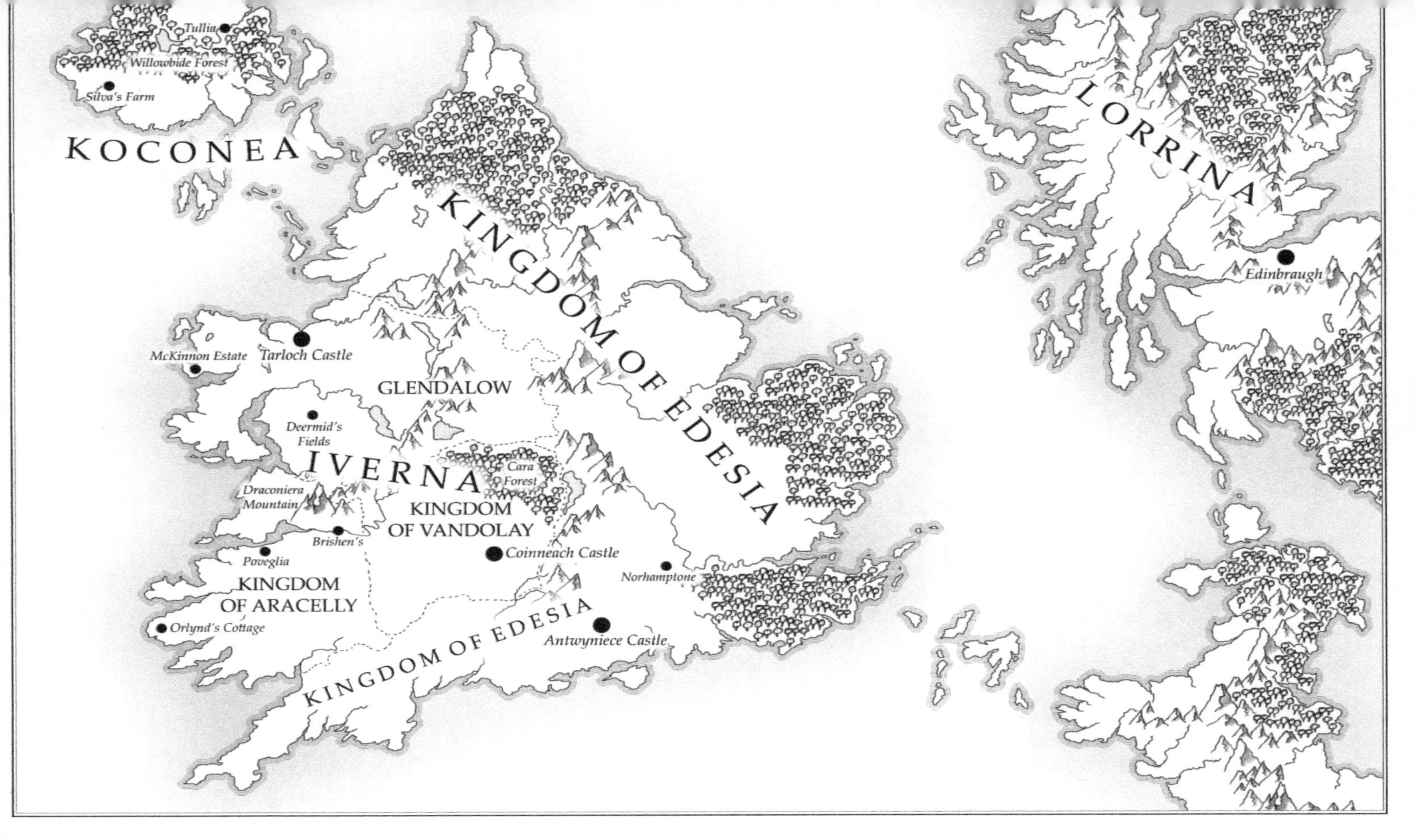

KOCONEA
Tullia
Willowbide Forest
Silva's Farm
LORRINA
Edinbraugh
KINGDOM OF EDESIA
McKinnon Estate
Tarloch Castle
GLENDALOW
Deermid's Fields
IVERNA
Cara Forest
Draconiera Mountain
KINGDOM OF VANDOLAY
Brishen's
Poveglia
Coinneach Castle
KINGDOM OF ARACELLY
Orlynd's Cottage
Norhamptone
KINGDOM OF EDESIA
Antwyniece Castle

# THE RITE OF RENEWAL

# THE RITE OF RENEWAL

## THE COUNTRY OF EDESIA

"Ah, Professor McKinnon, just in time. I trust you have been well. Please, sit." Mayor William's tone was formal but familiar. He pointed towards a tall-backed and weighty chair made from dark oak.

Mortain hesitated, checking the seat for crumbs and assessing its strength, a nervous habit he had picked up over the years. Finally, he nodded and sat, distracted by the ritual rather than the moment.

As he settled, he caught a fleeting glimpse of himself in the bevelled glass hanging by the door, hazy and half-lit in the flickering candlelight. The air in the room was cool, raising goosebumps along his arms despite his neat attire: a dark blue tunic draped over a crisp white shirt, light yellow breeches, and well-polished black boots. His brown hair was unruly, and he looked tired, his observant eyes, a blend of green, brown, and gold tones, darting anxiously. Mortain felt exposed. Every detail, the cold, and his untidy appearance reminded him how unsettled he was, especially when thinking of the country of Iverna, his birthplace.

"Mortain, I'd like to introduce you to Tiberius O'Brien." The mayor gestured, indicating a man in a priest's attire, who looked up, brushed his oily, shoulder-length black hair out of his face, and gave a polite wave.

Mortain nodded.

"By King John's authorisation, the council and I have appointed him leader of a religious quest in the land of Iverna. We believe a companion is needed."

Mortain tried to hide his discomfort, glancing towards the sunlight peeking out from rainclouds. "A companion? That would be perfectly splendid." His voice was tight, clearly hoping he wouldn't be chosen. "Certainly, you aren't suggesting me?" He laughed awkwardly, but the tension was obvious. When the mayor remained silent, he protested, clutching for any excuse. "But my students, they … they … need me for their exams.

Mayor William refused to be swayed. "Correct me if I am wrong, Mortain. You were born in the country of Iverna, were you not? Your family then relocated to Norhamptone in the country of Edesia when you were in your teens."

"Yes, but," Mortain began, glancing outside at the rain. Beneath his protest lay a deeper fear. The thought of returning home brought back too many memories. Iverna was where he had lost his own magic, his pride, and his sense of belonging. His adopted home, the country of Edesia, had become a refuge. The residents did not possess the gift of magic or care about the politics of Iverna. Here, Mortain had been given a chance to start anew. Going back to Iverna meant facing his past failures.

The mayor cut him off. "Then, I can think of no better candidate than you. Splendid. I've already sent a pigeon to the Kavanagh family. They possess a remarkable reputation in the craft and practice of apothecary. One of them will certainly be able to take over your duties here."

Mortain's jaw clenched, his brows drawing together as he scoffed, "A reputation doesn't mean one can teach."

He shook his head sharply; hands balled into fists in his lap. "I can't agree. No! I refuse to return!"

"There is no opportunity to refuse. By order of his Majesty, King John of Edesia, you are to pack your bags and make way to Iverna."

Mortain's hands shook, and his voice cracked: "You can't do this! The king does not know what I went through to reclaim my reputation or the dangers if I return!"

"The decision is final, Mortain, whether you approve of it or not."

Dread and helplessness tightened in Mortain's throat. He feared not only for his standing but for reopening long-buried wounds. The events forewarned by his Rite of Wands, an examination of the soul all witches and warlocks in Iverna endured to prove they had more than simply the strength to perform magic, were still happening, and he felt powerless to change his fate.

THE KINGDOM OF GLENDALOW—
TARLOCH TOWN—
IVERNA (2 YRS LATER)

TARLOCH TOWN stood in the kingdom of Glendalow, a realm of non-magical human residents. Merchants set up stalls along winding cobblestone streets, preparing for the Michaelmas festivities. The air, a mix of cool mist and intermittent sunlight, carried the scents of baked bread and roasted meat, mingling easily with laughter, chatter, and occasional disputes over market prices.

Children darted between vendors and crates of vegetables. Their play wove around barrels of wine and displays of autumn produce. Wisps of fog curled above the ground. In the early morning, townsfolk, draped in earth-toned garments that echoed practicality and tradition, moved purposefully. Some carried platters for the grand feast, others tended shops or herded livestock to the city square.

Michaelmas was more than a harvest celebration; it was a festival of gratitude and renewal, marked by blessings, music, and communal feasting. Locals adorned their stalls with garlands of rowan and holly, exchanging tokens of luck with their families to honour the belief that the archangel Michael protected their town from the harsh winter ahead.

Beneath the shadow of ancient stone walls, residents celebrated with a warmth that defied the brisk coastal air, weaving together memory and merriment as dusk approached and lanterns flickered to life along the winding streets. The celebration was abruptly interrupted by the sound of sharp, panicked whinnies from a horse that rose and broke, hooves hammering the ground in uneven, frantic bursts. Each strike sounded heavier than the last, making it seem like the horse was throwing its full weight into every stride.

"Help me!" cried a young man from his carriage, ample and ginger curly-haired, his round face flushed with panic, his frantic warning cutting through the jubilant noise. Moments earlier, brigand had attacked the man's family shop and ruined several barrels of wine. In the commotion, the horse, startled by shouts and flying debris, bolted, dragging the carriage away from the shop and into the bustling street.

With earnest, wide brown eyes, the man clung to the reins, his knuckles white. His simple, earth-toned vest and shirt, slightly rumpled from chaos, marked him as unassuming but sincere, as the horse-drawn carriage veered uncontrollably, scattering pedestrians and up-ending the market's orderly rhythm.

"Whoa! Oh, Dear Lord. Someone, please, help me!"

Mortain McKinnon, an apothecary known around the kingdom for his herbal concoctions and peculiar habits, also possessed rare knowledge of the magical world, even though he was merely a man. Never one to be caught without dried lavender or a pocket full of curious stones, he now absently twirled a sprig of rosemary between his fingers.

Upon hearing the man's shouts, Mortain looked up, his hazel eyes noticing the carriage careening towards him on the road. He instinctively patted himself down in a specific pattern, left pocket, right pocket, vest lining, trouser hem, searching for his wand, muttering under his breath about the importance of "wand discipline" and mentally ticking off a list of magical theories he recited to himself in times of stress. He reached into his pocket with the intention of casting a spell to make the horse stop, only to recall his pocket was empty.

Mortain's eyes grew wide; he remembered with sheer horror that he no longer possessed the ability to use one. He was not a warlock anymore. That magical gift had been stripped from him after he was charged with the crime of causing the accident that claimed the life of his master during his perfect apprenticeship.

How could life be so hollow without magic? Sometimes, closing his eyes, Mortain almost felt that old energy tingling in his fingertips, his wand, made from applewood, with an emerald crystal at the shaft, grasped in his hand. It was a wand of renewal, medical wisdom, and gentle authority. Now, only absence remained, an ache where purpose used to live. Every morning since the accident, shame and sorrow greeted him before the sun. Their shadows trailed him throughout the day. He couldn't shake the memory of his master's face nor the judgement in his mother's eyes. Magic was his purpose, his pride, his birthright. Now, stripped bare and marked by loss, he had wandered the past ten years through moments that never fit, haunted by one mistake he could not fix, and by what he will never again become.

"For God's sake, get out of the road!" He heard a shout from the direction of the out-of-control carriage.

As the carriage careened, barrels of wine soon were smashed, and food prepared for the upcoming feast was trampled. Anything unfortunate enough to be in the horse's path soon joined the jumbled mess.

"Hail Mary, full of grace. The Lord is with thee..." Mortain whispered, heart pounding as the carriage barrelled toward him.

He found himself staring forward, frozen, unable to move, still clutching his rosemary sprig. In moments of crisis, Mortain's mind often wandered to obscure prayers, overlapping in a jumble that could leave listeners baffled. Life at that very moment seemed to slow to a near standstill. His mind concluded that this was how his life was going to end, rather than the way his Rite of Wands had dictated. As he considered his demise, he thought there was nothing more tragic than being unable to be who he wanted to be.

*"Vorbíllion!"*

Mortain was abruptly lifted off the ground and thrown into a nearby trough. As he sat up, feeling the water soak through his tunic, he watched a beautiful woman step into the place where he'd been formerly standing.

The woman was wearing a dramatic, large black hat with a sweeping plume, reminiscent of early Regency high fashion. Her hair was long, wavy, and jet-black, styled in soft curls framing her face. Her attire featured a luxurious, dramatic dark gown designed to complement the iridescent blue-green hues of a labradorite pendant necklace. Under the gown, a voluminous white ruffled chemisette was visible, with rich vertical pleats and layered frills at the neckline.

She glanced over at Mortain, a brief flicker of concern passing across her features as she confirmed he was out of harm's way. For an instant, her green eyes narrowed, their pupils elongating to slitted shapes reminiscent of a serpent. Satisfied with her quick actions, she shifted her attention again towards the frantic horse and runaway carriage.

She reached out a hand, which was covered by an elegant light cream glove, in the direction of the carriage and shouted, *"Concye halímo!"*

The dark horse snorted and quickly halted.

"There, there. Shh," the woman spoke in a soothing voice, gently caressing the animal's nose.

The ginger-haired man's face lit up with relief. "Oh, thank ye, miss! Thought I'd never get out of that scrape!" His hands trembled slightly as he grasped Clarinda's arm in gratitude.

"You all right?" the woman asked, putting her wand away.

"Aye, I reckon so," said the man. "Just shaken up a bit. My name's Jasper. I was helpin' Pa with a delivery when the brigand attacked. It happened so fast. Them brigands spooked my horse. It took off runnin' and would not accept my orders! If you please, miss, I need to get back to me shop!" he said.

"I will accompany you. My name's Clarinda. I can help defend if those brigands decide to attack again."

Jasper nodded gratefully. "I cannot thank ye enough, miss. Afraid I do not know what would have happened if ye had not shown up when ye did."

"Ah, well, it's nothing, really." Clarinda smiled. "I just tend to show up when help is required, though I will admit it usually happens around the needs of children and mending torn clothing. We should travel by carriage. It will be faster than on foot. Jasper, you take the reins since you know the way."

"Aye, miss, but what about the mister?"

"Who?" Clarinda asked, a bit confused, her eyes lingering on Mortain for half a heartbeat longer than necessary. She watched as Jasper pointed over towards Mortain, the memory of her own recent heroics flickering between them like a secret. She observed the young man as he climbed out of the trough, his eyes wide with shock, a rawness that made him seem open and genuine in a way she found oddly compelling. "Oh! Not awkward. Well, a little awkward," she laughed to herself. "I'd forgotten I'd tossed him with my telekinesis."

"Telekinesis, miss? Is … is that some form of magic?" Jasper asked, raising a single eyebrow and slightly parting his mouth.

"Indeed. It is different from regular magic in that it doesn't require me to carry a wand to cast spells. Instead, I use my eyes!" Clarinda replied, looking towards Mortain. "Jasper, please, remain here. I must ensure that man's all right and apologise for getting him wet, before we travel to your shop."

"Aye, miss …" Jasper's voice trailed off, and a distant look settled over his features, as if he were momentarily lost in troubling thoughts.

As she approached Mortain, she heard the water dripping from his cloak, and from the rosemary sprig he was now examining with almost philosophical care.

"Hey! What's your name?" she called softly, her voice gentler than before, as if hoping to draw him out.

"Mortain," he answered through a mumble, but when he glanced at her, his guardedness faded. For a fleeting second, Clarinda caught a vulnerability in his eyes that mirrored her own. "You're a witch."

"Yes? And you are all wet," Clarinda answered, raising an eyebrow in playful challenge, her lips quirking with a hint of amusement. "Don't act as if you've never seen a witch from the kingdom of Aracelly in Glendalow before."

"I … uh … yes, yes, right." Mortain's face became bright red, his eyes flickering up to meet Clarinda's as if drawn by an unspoken gravity. He attempted to distract himself by wringing out his cloak, but found himself studying her eyes as they softened, their earlier intensity giving way to something quietly inviting. For a moment, Mortain felt utterly captured by her beauty, a feeling that unsettled and delighted him in equal measure.

"May I enquire what's so fascinating about that rose-mary sprig in your hand?" Clarinda teased, leaning just a bit closer, her gaze lingering. "You look at it as if you're expecting it to wilt!"

Mortain startled, nearly dropping it. "Oh! It is just, uh, a personal talisman I carry for use against misfortune," he replied, his voice trembling with the vulnerability of sharing a superstition. He risked a glance at Clarinda, hoping for understanding rather than ridicule.

Clarinda's lips formed into a gentle smile.

"I'd say that talisman of yours has assisted you on this day," Clarinda offered, her voice softer, the phrase carrying a kind of gentle approval.

"Indeed…" Mortain cleared his throat, courage blooming in the warmth of her regard. "You are not brandishing a wand in your hand. You must specialise in…"

"Telekinesis," they completed together, the word spoken in perfect sync. Their eyes met, just for an instant. Time seemed to slow, the air thick with sudden, mutual understanding. Neither needed to explain; a connection had sparked between them, as fleeting and profound as a magic spell.

"Sorry. I must get back to Jasper. He's the young man who almost killed you with his horse and carriage. A brigand attacked his family's shop, and his father may be injured."

Mortain's voice brimmed with gentle resolve as he stepped forward. "I will accompany you. I am an apothecary." Then, hesitating with a sheepish glance at his sodden attire, he added, "But first, I must find a proper change of clothing." The words hung between them, awkward yet earnest, a hint at his desire to remain close.

"No time for that," Clarinda replied, her eyes glinting mischievously. She retrieved from a hidden pocket a wand with a labradorite crystal at the shaft, and for a moment, Mortain wondered if she had read his mind.

"Hang on … is your wand made with rowan wood?" he asked, his curiosity laced with admiration.

"Indeed," Clarinda said. "Why? What would a non-magical man like yourself know about the business of wand crafting?" Her words were playful, but her eyes searched for his face with genuine interest.

As she raised her wand towards him, teasing, Mortain rushed to explain, nervous yet sincere. "I know wands made with rowan have never been used to commit evil!" He chuckled, hoping his knowledge might impress her, and as he held his hands up, droplets of water fell like confessions.

"Hum. I would not have imagined you would have had any interest in magical wand history. Stay still." She chanted, *"Parasicor."*

Mortain gasped as his clothing dried instantly, and a grin spread across his face. "May I dare say that was a bit of cheating?" he quipped, eyes twinkling with gratitude.

Clarinda rolled her eyes, but her amusement was genuine. She opened the carriage door, gesturing for him to enter. "Oh, do be quiet and get in." Secretly, she found Mortain's whimsical, almost childlike attitude toward the practicalities of magic oddly endearing, a quality that invited closeness.

Once the carriage was underway, Mortain, still buoyed by the warmth between them, asked, "What kind of shop does your family own, Jasper?"

Jasper straightened with a hint of pride, his eyes lighting up. "We specialise in drink, ye see. Ale, wine, mead..."

"I do see. And may I enquire what reason someone would have for attacking you or your family's shop?" Mortain asked, glancing sideways at Clarinda for her thoughts.

She met his gaze, and for a moment their eyes spoke volumes, the carriage feeling suddenly more intimate.

"The McMurrough family has been causing trouble in these areas since as early as I can remember," Clarinda replied, her words coloured by the kind of vulnerability that comes from sharing personal knowledge. "However, money would be the last of their concerns; rather, it would be the continuation of their outlaw ways. It seems, at times, they do these things just for the sake of doing them."

Mortain nodded, offering a subtle smile, a reassurance that she was not alone in her worries.

They continued west for about twenty minutes when the carriage abruptly stopped.

Mortain, caught off guard, was thrown from his side of the carriage and found himself face down right into Clarinda's lap. For a heartbeat, he felt her warmth beneath him, his cheeks blazing.

"I beg your pardon!" Mortain blushed, quickly sitting upright, but not before catching Clarinda's own amused smiles, sparkling with gentle affection.

"Shh!" Clarinda warned her finger to her lips. She listened for danger, her body tensed and close to Mortain's, a silent sense of partnership blossoming between them.

When Jasper did not respond, Clarinda opened the carriage door slowly, her posture protective.

Outside, heartbreak awaited. A river of wine and mead leaked from the inside of Jasper's family shop.

Clarinda stepped down from the carriage, but this time, Mortain followed with quiet attentiveness, drawn by her courage and compassion.

"That was me Granny's favourite wine. Cherry blossoms. Brewed right here in the cellar of our shop. Wasted. She would have a thing or two to say about this." Jasper's voice trembled, and both Mortain and Clarinda moved closer, sharing a look that acknowledged the sorrow of loss and the comfort found in company.

A slight moan caught their attention.

"Pa?" Jasper asked tentatively.

Mortain joined them, and all entered the shop. Several rough wooden shelves had been emptied of their wares. Broken bottles, both glass and ceramic, littered the ground, and wooden casks of mead had been broken open.

"Don't move!" Clarinda cautioned, her protective instincts shining through. She explored behind a small counter and found Jasper's father lying on the ground. The sight was sobering, and she turned to Mortain, her vulnerability on display: "He has been injured. Mortain, I could use your assistance."

Mortain nodded, his apothecary instincts taking over. He carefully examined the short, chubby man with curly white hair, noting a large, bald spot at the back of the scalp, covered in a mix of blood and what smelled like the remnants of cherry blossom wine.

He also caught Clarinda's gaze, with an intensity that felt like a caress. Their eyes met in silent conversation, philosophical questions passing between them: what does it mean to heal, to protect, to care for another?

"The brigands rendered him unconscious. Once this cut gets cleaned up, he should be fine, though he will have quite a headache."

Clarinda's voice was steady and warm as she knelt beside Jasper's father. "Let me help. I know what to do," she offered, determination glinting in her eyes.

"Here," Mortain said softly, handing a cloth to Clarinda, after he had cleaned the wound, their hands brushing. "Hold that over the bump on his head to help bring down the swelling."

The touch was brief but electric, a shared moment of vulnerability that sent warmth through Mortain's heart. Their fingers lingered for just a second longer than necessary, and Mortain, distracted by her presence, realised he was falling in love, their connection deepening with every shared glance and tender exchange.

It was not long after the two met that they decided to elope.

## THE KINGDOM OF ARACELLY—IVERNA

"AND I NOW pronounce you, Mr and Mrs McKinnon!" the priest announced to a room full of guests as Mortain and Clarinda kissed.

The wedding took place in a stone chapel adorned with woven garlands of ivy and wildflowers, their delicate scents mingling with the sweet aroma of burning peats from the hearth. Guests wore richly dyed woollen cloaks and linen tunics, their laughter echoing beneath the high, timbered ceiling. The ceremony was presided over by a priest in traditional vestments, who invoked blessings in both Latin and the local tongue.

After the vows were exchanged, the couple's hands were bound together in a symbolic handfasting, signifying their union. Musicians played lively reels on pipes and fiddles, and tables were laden with roasted meats, fresh bread, and honeyed wine, supplied by a thankful Jasper and father, all shared in communal celebration. The festivities often lasted well into the night, with storytelling, dancing, and songs passed down through generations, marking the joyous beginning of Mortain and Clarinda's life together.

At the wedding celebration, Mortain's eccentricity mingled with his joy. He became so wrapped up in a romantic moment with Clarinda that he forgot about important conversations with distinguished guests, leaving Tiberius holding his wine glass with an amused, knowing smile.

After the celebration had concluded, Tiberius approached Mortain.

"Congratulations! I am certain Clarinda will bring your family much joy and honour."

A grateful smile spread across Mortain's face. "Thank you, Your Eminence."

Tiberius leaned in with a glint of anticipation in his eyes. "I would like you to stop by my office. I have a proposition I am certain you will not be able to turn down."

"I would be more than happy to stop by, though may I inquire what this may be about?"

"Certainly. His Majesty, King Francis of Vandolay, I hear, needs a court physician. I have recommended you for the job. Your skill will serve him well."

"I … I don't rightly know…" He reached for a glass of wine from a server's tray as he passed by.

"How about your acceptance of the position?" Tiberius teased.

As Mortain lifted the glass to his lips, Clarinda turned towards him and smiled. "I can think of no better way to begin our lives together and provide for our children."

Mortain set his wine glass on a nearby table and, completely forgetting Tiberius, started to lead his new wife out of the room. "Then we shall consummate our marriage sooner rather than later."

Tiberius picked up Mortain's wine glass and, with a small, knowing smile, turned back to the celebration.

As the evening waned and laughter echoed through the grand hall, Mortain lingered in quiet thought. The path behind him had been filled with uncertainty, marked by moments of courage and love that had brought him here. Now, with Clarinda by his side and the promise of new beginnings, he could not help but wonder about the future and the tremendous amount of anxiety he felt.

Mierta, their son, whose arrival marked the dawn of hope and the shadow of duty — a blessing and burden, inseparably entwined. It was whispered in Mortain's Rite of Wands that Mierta would one day serve as the apothecary destined to save Iverna from the Shreya, a devastating bubonic plague.

This destiny meant Mierta's life would be shaped by expectations and responsibilities far beyond those of an ordinary child. These words of prophecy trembled in Mortain's heart, mingling pride with apprehension.

He glanced at Clarinda, her presence bright and steady, and silently vowed to guide and protect their family while preparing for the challenges yet to come and the legacy their son would inherit.

# THE STORY CONTINUES
## IN THE RITE OF WANDS

**Perfect for fans wanting hope and healing in a story about loss, sacrifice, and becoming whole again.**

*The Rite of Wands* is a Celtic medieval epic fantasy series that's being called, "*Game of Thrones* in Ireland during the Black Plague, starring Matt Smith".

**A Celtic medieval kingdom…A neurodivergent apothecary…And a prophecy of fate**

As an apothecary, Mierta McKinnon has fought death with herbs, discipline, and grit. But prophecy doesn't care how hard you work. It only cares about what it can get.

When Mierta undergoes the Rite of Wands, a ritual designed to awaken him as a warlock, he discovers he has been prophesied to save the land of Iverna from a devastating bubonic plague known as the Shreya. Or succumb to it.

Burdened by this knowledge, Mierta struggles to become the warlock he must be, questioning his strength, value, and worth. His only chance of survival lies in navigating a treacherous web of manipulation and forbidden magic before the knowledge of the future destroys him and the world he strives to save.

But in a court where prophecy is currency, being "chosen" is just another way to be owned.

# PLEASE WRITE A REVIEW

*Dear friend,*

Thank you for reading! If you enjoyed this book, please take a few moments to rate and review so that you can help others make informed decisions on whether my books are right for them. Thank you!

*~ Mackenzie*

REVIEW.THERITEOFRENEWALBOOK.COM

# ACKNOWLEDGMENTS

100 Covers for the cover design

BookHelpline for handling the editing and taking my writing to a new level

Chris Walker-Thomson for returning to narrate the audiobooks

Dewi Hargreaves for having the skill to take my terrible Photoshop map and transform it into something amazing!

*DoctorWhoOnline* for reconnecting me with my target audience!

Donna Lutkus-Phillips for encouragement to never give up, despite what challenge life threw at me!

JV Arts for the creation of the interior graphics

LD for connecting me with the right people to teach me the business side of publishing!

Lynne Smith for the inspiration behind the character of Clarinda.

# ABOUT THE AUTHOR

Mackenzie Flohr is a multi-award-winning fantasy author whose work has earned international acclaim.

A native of Strongsville, Ohio, Mackenzie grew up immersed in imagination, developing a lifelong fascination with myth, magic, and the resilience of the human spirit. Her writing is known for its immersive world-building and character-driven exploration of identity, courage, and overcoming life's challenges.

Her published works include *The Whispered Tales of Graves Grove* (BHC Press, 2017), *Unknown Realms* (Fiction-Atlas Press, 2019), *The Binge Watcher's Guide to Doctor Who: A History of Doctor Who and the First Female Doctor* (Riverdale Avenue Books, 2019), and *The Companions of Doctor Who* (Fayetteville Mafia Press, 2024).

Mackenzie resides in Michigan, where she writes tales to enchant, inspire, and ignite imagination.

Visit Mackenzie's website at:
*www.mackenzieflohr.com*